THE
WHEAT
DOLL

ALISON L. RANDALL

Illustrated by
BILL FARNSWORTH

PEACHTREE
ATLANTA

It was hot in the valley. Mary Ann wiped her forehead and grabbed the carrot top again. But the fat carrot bottom still refused to budge from the ground.

"This is going to take forever, Betty," Mary Ann sighed.

Betty didn't answer. She never did. The only sound she ever made was the *swish-shush* of her wheat-filled body. But Mary Ann knew the doll was listening.

"Sorry, Betty. I need more room for the carrots," Mary Ann said. She pulled the doll from her apron pocket and set her on a stump near the garden. Betty sat up straight and still. Her embroidery eyes never blinked, but Mary Ann knew she was paying attention.

Betty watched as Mary Ann made her way up the row of carrots, tugging them out one by one.

Finally, when Mary Ann's pockets were full, she gathered up her apron tightly and headed for the root cellar.

She didn't notice the black clouds spilling over the mountains, or the air growing heavy.

As Mary Ann emptied the carrots into the cool dark of the cellar, her mama called her into the cabin.

"Mary Ann, hurry! Come help me with these cracks." She handed her daughter a bundle of rags.

"But, Mama—" Mary Ann began, remembering Betty on the stump.

"No buts," her mama said firmly. "There's a storm brewing."

Hastily, Mary Ann tore the rags into smaller pieces. She stuffed them between the logs of her family's cabin, wherever a bit of sky peeked through. With luck, the rags would keep out the dust and damp of the storm.

A strong gale of wind whooshed across the valley. It tore through the garden and ripped at the corn stalks. It knocked poor Betty straight off the stump and tumbled her head over heels down a hill. She came to rest in a rocky hole at the bottom.

Back in the cabin, Mary Ann finished stuffing the cracks. But before she could race to the garden, Papa blew through the door with another gust of wind. Behind him, the day had turned dark as night. "Storm's a bad one," he said.

"Oh, no!" Mary Ann cried. "Betty's out in the garden!"

"Well, you can't go look for her now," Papa said.

"I have to," Mary Ann insisted, but Mama's thin, strong arms held her back.

"You'll do no such thing," she said.

Outside, the pounding rain soaked Betty's body. The wheat inside her began to swell. Suddenly, a gush of mud broke loose from the hill and poured over Mary Ann's doll. She lay trapped under a gooey blanket, hidden from sight.

The storm seemed to last forever. As soon as it had passed, Mary Ann raced out the door. The garden looked as if a giant broom had swept through it.

Mary Ann rushed to the stump where she had left Betty.

Her best friend was gone!

Mary Ann searched everywhere—behind the stump, under the corn stalks, and down the hill.

"Betty!" she called frantically, again and again. "Where are you?"

15

Up and down the rows Mary Ann went, calling and hunting, the garden blurred by her tears. Almost before she knew it, night began to fall.

She couldn't find Betty anywhere.

A lantern bobbed toward Mary Ann. Her papa stepped through the dark and wrapped her in his broad, warm arms.

"Time to come in," he said.

The days and months passed, but Mary Ann never gave up looking for Betty. The winter seemed very long without her best friend. She missed the *swish-shush* of her doll's wheat body, and her apron pocket felt as empty as her heart. There were chores to do, but now there was no Betty to sit and watch while she dipped candles and braided rags into rugs.

When Mary Ann worked on her embroidery, it reminded her of Betty's satin stitch eyes, chain stitch mouth, and lazy daisy ears.

When she walked to the schoolhouse, listening to the other girls' chatter reminded her of the one friend she could always trust to keep her secrets.

At last, the long winter gave way to spring. Mary Ann took a basket and headed to the garden plot. It was planting season, time to sprinkle the tiny carrot seeds into their rows. She wished Betty could be there to watch the feathery greens poke through the brown earth.

Mary Ann tried hard not to think about Betty. She stood on the stump and breathed in the fresh spring air.

That's when she saw something green and spiky growing in the mud at the bottom of the hill. She hopped off the stump and ran down the slope to see.

A small patch of slender shoots had sprouted in the mud. The patch had a funny shape. It had arms and legs and a head. Could it be…?

Mary Ann ran her fingers across the tender grass. "Betty?" she whispered. "Is that you?"

The thin blades seemed to sigh at her touch. And Mary Ann knew that Betty was listening.

All summer long, Mary Ann tended the patch of wheat until the green shoots grew tall and turned to gold. She cut the stalks and harvested the kernels of grain. Then she set to work sewing and stitching. She took special care with Betty's new eyes and ears.

Mary Ann had lots to tell Betty, and she knew that her friend would be listening.

More About Mary Ann

In the late 1800s, in the territory of Utah, a young girl named Mary Ann Winters lost her wheat doll. Frontier children didn't have fancy toys. Girls used whatever they had to make their dolls. Rag dolls, like Betty, were made from fabric scraps and stuffed with anything that was on hand—rags, sawdust, or horsehair. Mary Ann used wheat to fill her doll, most likely because that's what her family grew on their farm. I don't know the real name of Mary Ann Winters's doll or how it was lost. I don't know if Mary Ann made a new doll later. However, I do know that she never forgot the wondrous moment the next spring when she found her doll growing as a patch of new wheat. How do I know that? Because she told her children about it. And her children told their children. And so forth, on down until one of Mary Ann's descendants told me, the author of this story. When I heard it, I knew it needed to be shared. My thanks to Mary Ann's descendants, who agreed.

—*Alison L. Randall*

To Kaylene, for sharing,

and

to Jeff, for everything else

—A. L. R.

For Fran

—B. F.

Published by
PEACHTREE PUBLISHERS
1700 Chattahoochee Avenue
Atlanta, Georgia 30318-2112
www.peachtree-online.com

Text © 2008 by Alison Randall
Illustrations © 2008 by Bill Farnsworth

Book and cover design by Loraine M. Joyner
Composition by Melanie McMahon Ives
Illustrations created in oil on canvas

Printed in February 2010 in China by Imago
Dongguan, Guangdong
10 9 8 7 6 5 4 3 2

Library of Congress Cataloging-in-Publication Data

Randall, Alison L.
  The wheat doll / written by Alison L. Randall ; illustrated by Bill
Farnsworth.-- 1st ed.
     p. cm.
  Summary: On the nineteenth-century Utah frontier, Mary Ann is
heartbroken when her doll Betty is lost during a fierce storm and her
sadness lasts all winter long, until spring brings a wonderful surprise.
  ISBN-13: 978-1-56145-456-3 / ISBN-10: 1-56145-456-7
  [1. Dolls--Fiction. 2. Lost and found possessions--Fiction. 3.
Storms--Fiction. 4. Frontier and pioneer life--Utah--Fiction. 5.
Utah--History--19th century--Fiction.] I. Farnsworth, Bill, ill. II.
Title.
  PZ7.R15538Whe 2008
  [Fic]--dc22   2008004562